D1275600

For Jenny and Michael
with love from
J. A.

For David, Brigitte, Chlöe, Christof, and Dimitri
T. H.

The author and publisher wish to thank
Martin Jenkins for his invaluable assistance
in the preparation of this book.

Text copyright © 1993 by Judy Allen
Illustrations copyright © 1993 by Tudor Humphries

First U.S. edition 1994
First published in Great Britain in 1993 by Walker Books Ltd., London.

Library of Congress Cataloging-in-Publication Data

Allen, Judy.
Seal / Judy Allen ; illustrated by Tudor Humphries.—
1st U.S. ed.
Summary: While vacationing in Greece, Jenny discovers a secluded
beach where a rare seal hides his family. Includes information about the seal
species and environmental threats.
ISBN 1-56402-145-9
[1. Seals (Animals)—Fiction.  2. Wildlife conservation—Fiction.  3. Greece—Fiction.]
I. Humphries, Tudor, ill.  II. Title.
PZ7.A4273Se     1993       93-3642

10 9 8 7 6 5 4 3 2 1

Printed in Hong Kong

The pictures in this book were done in watercolor.

Candlewick Press
2067 Massachusetts Avenue
Cambridge, Massachusetts 02140

# SEAL

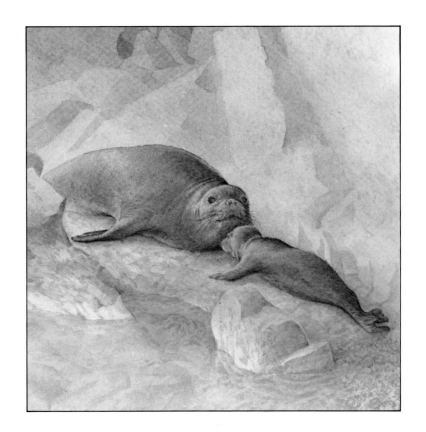

by
## Judy Allen
illustrated by
## Tudor Humphries

## CANDLEWICK PRESS
CAMBRIDGE, MASSACHUSETTS

"One day," said Jenny, "I want to know something that none of you know." She was on vacation in Greece with her mother, her father, and her big brother Joe. Every day, for almost two weeks, the three of them had told her things. They had told her stories about the ancient Greek gods. They had explained how the ruined temples and broken statues had once looked. They had shown her little white churches, huge hillside monasteries, and trees growing olives and lemons. They had taught her how to eat an artichoke and how to recognize a swallowtail butterfly, a spider crab, and a stinging jellyfish.

Now, sitting outside a café eating honey cakes, Jenny decided that her head was so full it didn't have room for a single extra piece of information.

Her father pointed across the small harbor to an island that rose from the sea like a miniature mountain.

"We must get a caïque to take us out there," he said. "Jenny, a caïque is a kind of boat."

Jenny put her hands over her ears. "Don't tell me anything more!" she said.

"You shouldn't mind us knowing more than you," said her mother. "We're all older than you are."

"But you'll always be older than me," said Jenny. "I'll never catch up."

Later, down by the boats that were moored in the shallows, Jenny's father talked with two fishermen. The older one spoke only Greek. His son Stefanos, though, could speak English. Stefanos was friendly, but he shook his head when Jenny's father asked about a trip to the island.

"It is only a rock," he said. "No one goes there."

"We'd like to have a picnic on it," said Jenny's mother.

"Not possible," said Stefanos. "There are many other rocks under the sea around it. The bottom

would be torn out of my boat. Instead
I will take you night-fishing, if you
would like?"

"We would like!" said Joe.

"Then we go tonight," said
Stefanos cheerfully.

The evening sun was still making a glowing red path across the sea when they got into the boat, but Stefanos lit the lamps at once. They hissed softly as they burned.

"They're gas lamps," said Joe. "That's why they make that sound."

Jenny ignored him.

"They are called *pyrofania*," said Stefanos. "That means fire crowns."

Jenny smiled. She liked the name—and she found that she didn't mind Stefanos telling her things.

His boat had an engine, but he didn't use it. He rowed out on the darkening sea.

Jenny's mother pointed back toward the land, where a thousand tiny glimmerings flickered among the shadowy trees.

"Fireflies!" she said.

But Jenny was looking in the other direction. "I can see a silver seal," she said.

"Are there seals in Greece?" said Jenny's father.

"Not silver ones!" said her mother.

"Where is it?" said Joe.

"It's gone now," said Jenny.

Stefanos said nothing. He stopped rowing and lowered a net into the water. "We may get fish here," he said. "They come to the light."

"There!" said Jenny, half standing up and making the boat rock. "There it is!"

Something pearly white was moving toward them, trailing shimmering streaks through the water.

"Jenny's right—it *is* a seal," said Joe.

"It isn't really silver," said his father as the seal submerged. "There's phosphorescence in the water." He began to explain about the microscopic sea creatures that glow almost as brightly as fireflies, but Jenny wasn't listening. "Where's it gone?" she said.

"They are rare and shy," said Stefanos. "I think it will go far away."

"Well spotted, Jen," said Joe.

Jenny hardly saw the little shoal of whitebait they caught that night, or the small octopus. She stared at the sea until Stefanos rowed them back to the harbor—but the silver seal did not appear again.

When she saw it the next day it no longer looked silver—
it was brown and glossy. She stood at the edge of the sea,
near Stefanos and his father, who were sorting their nets,
and watched it through her mother's binoculars.

Joe tried to interest her in a row of octopuses hanging
out to dry in the sun, but Jenny took no notice of him,
and he wandered off.

"They all tell me things," she complained to Stefanos.

"I give you something to tell them," said Stefanos. "Your
seal is a monk seal."

His father spoke angrily. Stefanos shook his head and pointed to a boat on the horizon. "He says the seals take our fish," he explained to Jenny. "I tell him it is the big fishing boats that do that."

The old man grumbled again. "He says the seals get caught in the nets and tear them," said Stefanos. "That is true, but it doesn't happen often."

"Do the seals get out of the nets again?" said Jenny.

"Sometimes," said Stefanos.

"But sometimes they drown."

Later, Jenny got frightened and called out to Stefanos. "My seal dived," she said, "and he hasn't come up again. He must be caught in a net."

"They stay underwater for a long time," said Stefanos.

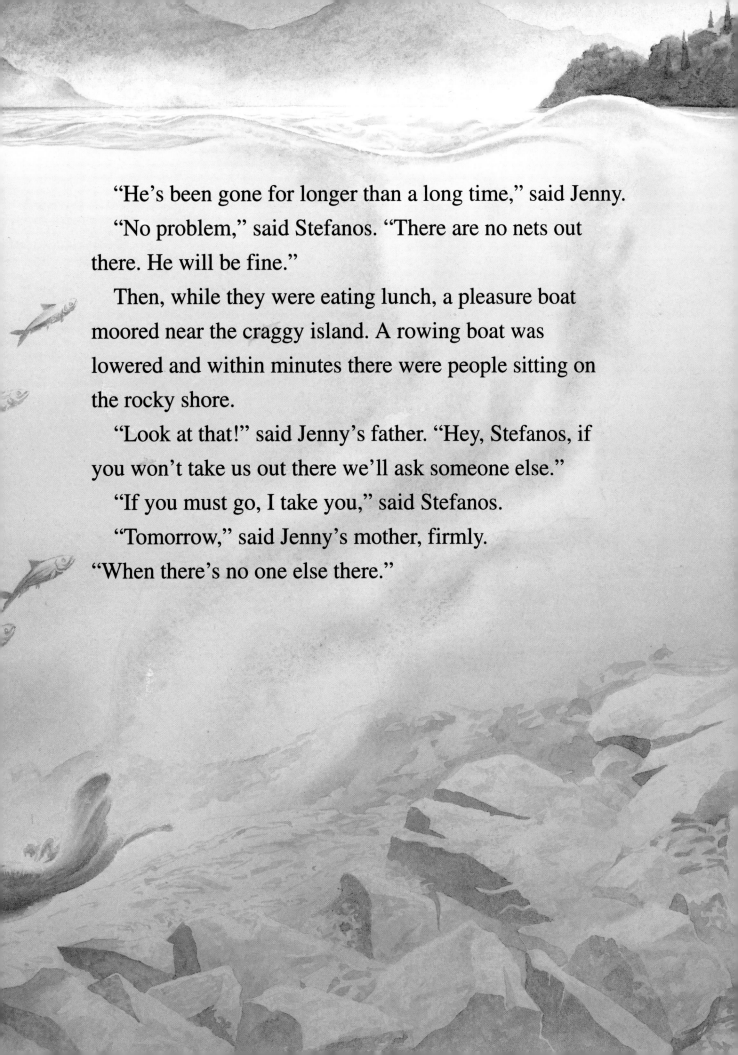

"He's been gone for longer than a long time," said Jenny.

"No problem," said Stefanos. "There are no nets out there. He will be fine."

Then, while they were eating lunch, a pleasure boat moored near the craggy island. A rowing boat was lowered and within minutes there were people sitting on the rocky shore.

"Look at that!" said Jenny's father. "Hey, Stefanos, if you won't take us out there we'll ask someone else."

"If you must go, I take you," said Stefanos.

"Tomorrow," said Jenny's mother, firmly. "When there's no one else there."

They went in the morning, with a bag of food and a
bundle of beach towels. The tiny island was farther
away than they had realized, and this time Stefanos
used the engine. When they drew near, though, he shut it off.

"I cannot go closer," he said.

Looking down through the clear water, Jenny saw
tiny fish swimming among the dark rocks that grew
out of the sandy seabed.

Her father jumped out first. The water reached
almost to his waist. "Come on, Jen," he said,
"I'll give you a piggyback."

Joe balanced the picnic bag on his head and his mother
held the towels high. Stefanos watched them wade ashore.
"I will be nearby, fishing," he called. "Any time you say,
I will take you to a beautiful beach."

"He really doesn't like people coming here, does he?"
said Jenny's father quietly. "I can't imagine why."

He found a flat rock to lie on while his shorts dried.
Jenny's mother found a pool full of sea anemones.
Joe found two caves. The sun shone through a hole
in the roof of one, but the other was shady enough to
keep the picnic cool.

Stefanos rowed a little way off and lowered baskets to
catch squid.

Jenny clambered to the top of the rock island to watch
for her seal. After a little while, Joe passed her lunch up
to her—bread, crumbly goat's cheese, an enormous tomato,
and some cherries.

Suddenly the seal appeared from nowhere, making her
jump. It looked straight at her, then dived. This time
Jenny had a good view, and though she stared for so long
that she dribbled tomato seeds down her front,
it did not come up again.

There must be a cave under the island, Jenny thought.
She left the remains of her lunch and crossed the top
of the island to the slope on the other side.

She could see Stefanos in his boat, but she couldn't
tell if he was watching her. Her family was too busy
eating to look up. She lay on her stomach and stared
down—and a sleek head popped out of the water
below her. For a moment she was only a couple of feet
from the sad, whiskery face, and then the seal somersaulted
and sent up a flurry of sand. When the sand settled, the
seal was gone.

You definitely have a cave, thought Jenny, but I'm not
following you underwater to find it. Then she remembered
Joe's first cave with the hole in the roof. Perhaps this one
is the same, she thought.

It didn't take her long to find the jagged
opening, half hidden by a little
scrubby bush. She knelt
down and peered
through it.

At first all she could see was a
pattern of shimmering green and gold. Then she
could make out a huge, dim cavern, with a stony floor
and shelves of rock. The sun shone through the shallow
sea and in at the underwater opening, lighting everything
with a watery glow.

There was a movement at the edge of the water, and the
seal appeared, hauling himself out of the water and onto the
little pebbly cave-beach. Higher up, where the sea did not
reach, three more seals were resting—and two of them had
babies, lying close. Jenny could hear the sighing of the sea
and the soft bleating of one of the seal pups.

For what seemed like a hundred years she crouched
there, enchanted. Then she realized that, at last,
she knew something that not one of the rest
of her family knew.

She stood up—and saw that Stefanos was bringing his boat closer, shouting and waving. "There is a squall coming," he called. "You must come—I have to get my boat in to harbor."

In the rush, Jenny had no time to say anything, especially as Joe carried her out first, then waded back to help the others collect their belongings.

Stefanos kept the boat steady and spoke to her softly. "I know what you found," he said. "Their last hiding place. I must tell you that if they are disturbed the mothers may abandon the babies, or even kill them."

"I didn't disturb them," said Jenny, horrified.

"No," said Stefanos, "but will you betray them?"

"My family wouldn't hurt them!" said Jenny.

"Wouldn't they want to look?" said Stefanos. "Wouldn't they dive down, just once? And wouldn't others hear of it, and come out to see?"

"But I *really* want to tell them," said Jenny, as the family waded toward them.

"I understand," said Stefanos. "I give you something else to tell, instead." He thought for a moment. Then, "Hundreds of years ago," he said, "people believed that a tent made of sealskin would protect them from lightning."

Jenny frowned.

"And," said Stefanos, "they believed that if they dragged the skin of a seal around a field the crops would not be damaged by hailstones."

Jenny looked back at her family, wading out toward the boat.

"Will you keep the secret?" said Stefanos. "For the seals?" Then he turned to help the others on board.

The water became choppier and the rain began to fall as they traveled back. Jenny sat very quiet, very still.

"Someone doesn't mind the bad weather," said Jenny's father, as the seal's head broke the surface behind the boat.

"It's always alone, isn't it?" said her mother.

"I can tell you something none of you know," said Jenny.

"What?" said Joe.

Jenny told the story about the sealskin and the lightning.

"What an extraordinary thing," said her mother.

"How did you find that out?" said her father.

Jenny looked at them. They were all listening to her with interest. She couldn't remember that they had ever done that before. "I can tell you something else, too," she said.

Stefanos watched her. The seal sank below the surface, leaving a ring of water.

Jenny drew a deep breath. Then she told the story about the sealskin and the hailstones. "That's all," she said.

Stefanos smiled broadly. "Believe me," he said, "Jenny is wiser than you know."

# SEAL FACT SHEET

The Mediterranean monk seal is the rarest seal in the world. In ancient times many thousands of them used to live in the Mediterranean and off the North African coast in the Atlantic. Now there may be as few as five hundred and certainly no more than seven hundred altogether, and the number gets smaller every year. Most of the seals live around the Greek islands of the Aegean, but there are still some in the Atlantic. As well as the Mediterranean monk seals, there used to be two other sorts of monk seals. Sadly, the Caribbean monk seal became extinct about thirty years ago, but the Hawaiian monk seal still survives in the Pacific Ocean and is doing better than the Mediterranean monk seal.

## WHAT ARE THE DANGERS FOR MEDITERRANEAN MONK SEALS?

Fishermen have persecuted monk seals for hundreds of years, because they think they damage fishing nets and eat too many fish. They have shot the seals, left them to drown in nets, and dynamited the caves where they have their young. Tourist developments have destroyed many good breeding sites, and tourist boats often disturb the mothers and young. The seals are very sensitive to disturbance, and the mother finds it very difficult to raise her pups when this happens.

## IS ANYONE HELPING MEDITERRANEAN MONK SEALS?

Yes. Concerned scientists and organizations have tried to find ways to stop fishermen from killing monk seals and have tried to persuade governments to set up sanctuaries for the seals.

## ARE EFFORTS TO SAVE MEDITERRANEAN MONK SEALS SUCCEEDING?

Unfortunately not very well. The population seems to be getting smaller every year. Even where the seals are not persecuted by people they may suffer from natural accidents. For instance, off the coast of Mauritania in North Africa in the 1980s, many seals were killed when a cave fell in on top of them.

## WHAT CAN YOU DO TO HELP?

For more information about seals and what you can do to help them, write to the following address:

The Marine Mammal Center
Marin Headlands
Golden Gate National Recreation Area (GGNRA)
Sausalito, California 94965

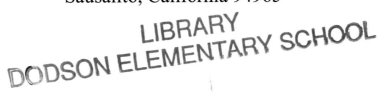